ISLAND HERITAGE™
PUBLISHING
A DIVISION OF THE MADDEN CORPORATION

94-411 Kō'aki Street
Waipahu, Hawai'i 96797-2806
Orders: (800) 468-2800
Information: (808) 564-8800
Fax: (808) 564-8877
ISLANDHERITAGE.COM

ISBN: 1-61710-306-3
First Edition, First Printing—2016
COP 161706

PEEKABOO
the Poi Dog

Written by Wendy Kunimitsu Haraguchi
Illustrated by Kat Uno

ISLAND HERITAGE™
PUBLISHING

Peekaboo the poi dog was
as bored as she could be,

For it was pouring rain
outside her home in Waikīkī.

She looked around at all her toys
(and she had quite a few!)

But today she wished that she could
seek out something really new.

2

She asked her mom, "What can
I do? The day has just begun."

Her mom replied, "Do what I say,
and you'll have lots of fun.

"Close your eyes, and spin around,
and slowly count to three.

After that, just pick up the
first thing that you see.

"Then imagine that it's something else...
like a double hull canoe.

Be as creative as you can.
Let's see what you can do!"

Peekaboo Soon followed
through and gave a happy howl

Because her paw was holding up
her favorite beach towel.

At first, her mind was just a
blank, but then sure enough,

Ideas started flowing freely.
This game would not be tough!

The towel became a picnic
blanket under a coconut tree,

Where she chased some hungry
mynah birds away from her musubi.

Next it was her cape when
she was Super Peekaboo,

Rescuing someone blown off
Pali Lookout as she flew.

Now it was her sail as
she windsurfed in Kailua,

While her beach friends sculpted
up a huge sand manapua.

Next it was her parachute
while diving in the sky.

She watched the surfers at
North Shore ride waves 30 feet high.

Now it was a warm scarf as
she skied swiftly down the snow,

Avoiding Mauna Kea's sharp,
volcanic rocks below.

Then it was her kayak on
Kaua'i's coastal waves.

She paddled next to monk seals,
waterfalls, and caves.

Soon it was her ti-leaf skirt,
as she swayed around with grace

At the Hawai'i Hula Festival.
She even won first place!

On Maui, she was hovering
beneath a parasail,

When water spouted on her legs
from a breaching humpback whale.

Then she started flying
on a magic goza mat,

From Diamond Head to Ka'ena Point
in just ten seconds flat!

Next it was her race flag
at the starting position

Of a friendly nēnē goose
waddling competition.

Now it was a camping tent
at Bellows Field Beach Park.

She played the ʻukulele and
caught sand crabs in the dark.

Last it was a hammock gently
swaying from two trees,

As she enjoyed a rainbow
shave ice in the Hale'iwa breeze.

Peekaboo Soon noticed that
the day had passed by fast.

She hugged and thanked her mom
and said, "I really had a blast!

"Now I know that my
imagination is the key

To many new adventures
that are awaiting me!"

The End

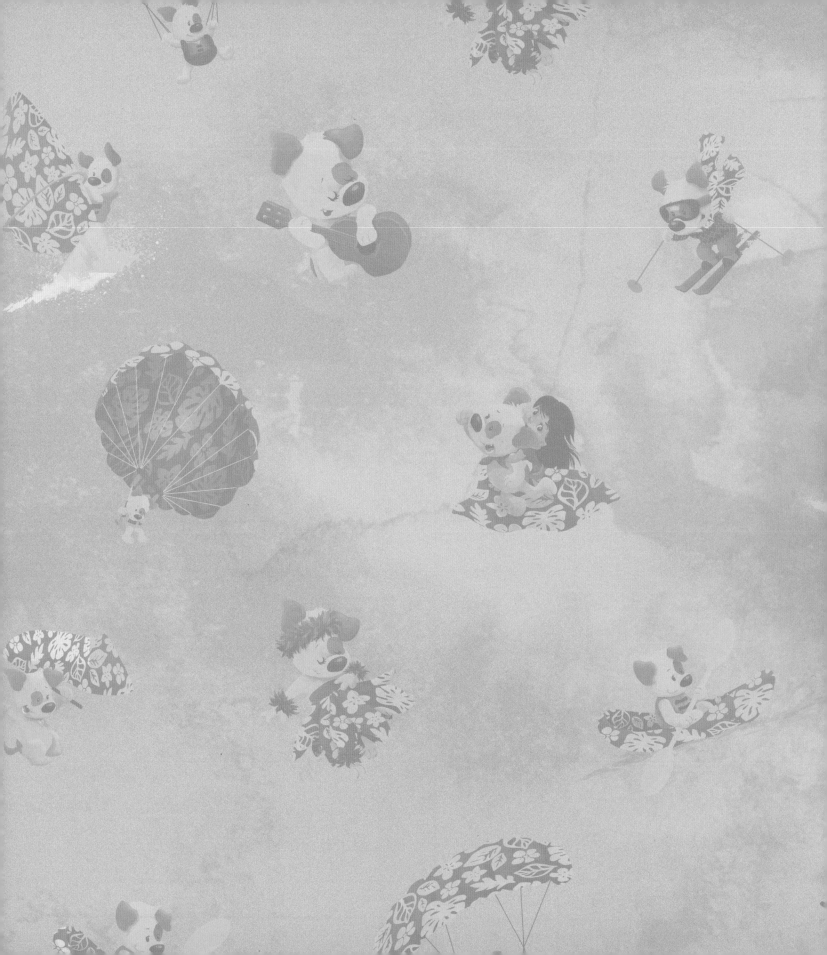